TO FOUR FUNNY HOTDOGS—
SUMMER, LEON, LUC AND XAVIER—A.D

TO MY LOVING WIFE, CLARE, AND MY
AWESOME PARENTS, ELAINE AND BILL—D.M

Scholastic Children's Books
An imprint of Scholastic Ltd
Euston House, 24 Eversholt Street, London, NW1 1DB, UK
Registered office: Westfield Road, Southam, Warwickshire, CV47 0RA
SCHOLASTIC and associated logos are trademarks and/or
registered trademarks of Scholastic Inc.

Hot Dog! first published by Scholastic Australia, 2016
Text copyright © Anh Do, 2016
Illustrations by Dan McGuiness, copyright © Scholastic Australia, 2016
Cover and internal design by Nicole Stofberg

Hot Dog! 2: Party Time first published by Scholastic Australia, 2017
Text copyright © Anh Do, 2017
Illustrations by Dan McGuiness, copyright © Scholastic Australia, 2017
Cover and internal design by Nicole Stofberg

This collection first published in the UK by Scholastic Ltd, 2019

The right of Anh Do to be identified as the author of this work has been asserted.

ISBN 978 1407 19928 3

A CIP catalogue record for this book
is available from the British Library.

Printed by
Papers used by Scholastic Children's Books are made
from wood grown in sustainable forests.

1 3 5 7 9 10 8 6 4 2

This is a work of fiction. Names, characters, places, incidents
and dialogues are products of the author's imagination or are used
fictitiously. Any resemblance to actual people, living or dead,
events or locales is entirely coincidental.

www.scholastic.co.uk

ANH DO

ILLUSTRATED BY
DAN McGUINESS

HOT DOG!

■SCHOLASTIC

ONE

If you're thinking this book is about the yummy hotdog that you eat, then you're thinking of **the wrong hotdog!**

THIS thing will <u>NOT</u> be going on any adventures!

If you're thinking of the **super cute, super short, barking** type of hotdog . . . then you've come to the right place!

I'm **Hotdog!** I'm a **sausage dog**, which means my legs are **short**, and I have a **really l-o-o-o-n-g body.**

Keep going.

There you go!

This morning I woke up with a **very blocked nose.**

It was **so blocked** I couldn't smell my breakfast!

SNIFF!

NOTHING...

I couldn't **smell** my toothpaste.

I couldn't even **smell** my feet!

SNIFF!

NOTHING. . .

But that's actually a pretty good thing. Feet **never** smell good!

Being a dog with very short legs is really good for lots of things, like playing **hide-and-seek . . .**

And **sleeping** . . .

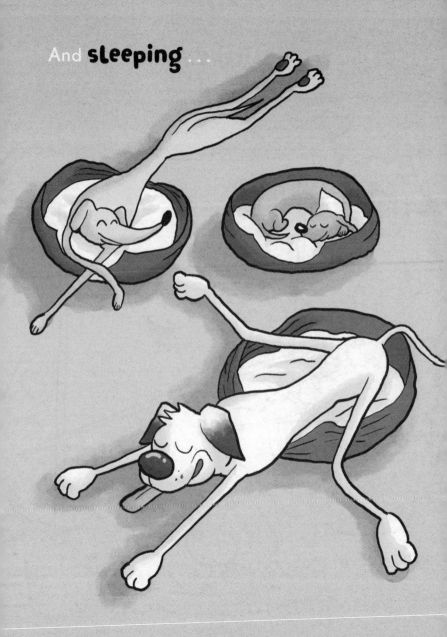

Or dancing the **Limbo**...

But having short legs also makes it **hard** to do lots of things ... like **tying my shoelaces.**

Or **racing** . . .

SWOOSH!

LEAP!

CLUNK!

Or **playing guitar**...

But that's OK, I usually figure out **another way** to do things.

That's the thing about me, I like to **keep on trying**. No matter what!

And today, I was going to try and **fly my kite**. Let's see if **my friends** want to join in!

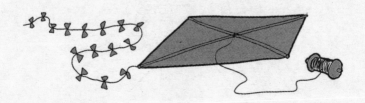

TWO

We were supposed to be meeting Lizzie right here by the **big pine tree.**

WHERE IS SHE?

Oh, there she is. "Oops, sorry Lizzie."
Lizzie's a lizard that can **blend in**
with almost anything.

She can blend into a **brick wall**...

BOO!

Or a **bunch of bananas** . . .

The worst is when she blends in with a **doorway**.

OOF!

We were both looking around the park,
trying to see if **Kevin** was here yet.
Kev's always a bit **slow** to show up ...

All we could see was this
weird-looking cow.

MOO!

Suddenly **the cow** waddled over.

"You guys, it's me, _Kevin_," said Kevin.

His humans must have **dressed him up** again. They **love** sticking him in **crazy costumes**!

Kevin dressed up as a shark.

Kevin dressed up as Santa.

Sometimes they even dress Kevin up
as Kevin.

Kevin dressed up as Kevin.

Here's the thing you **need to know**
about Kevin . . .

He is the **laziest living thing** on earth.

Here's how his humans take him **"for a walk"**.

At home, he has a **grabbing tool** that he uses to reach things.

Like his **dinner bowl** ...

... or his **undies**.

He even has a **grabbing tool** he uses to reach his **grabbing tool**.

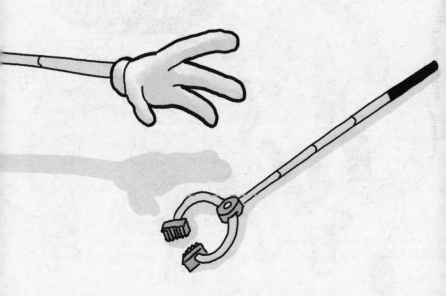

"That's a **really** bad outfit," said Lizzie.

"Go ahead and **laugh**," said Kev. "Just remember that cats are related to lions, the **king of the beasts**."

NOTHING WILL TAKE AWAY MY PRIDE!

As he said that, a **yellow fluffy thing** fell right on his head.

"Aw look," said Lizzie, "it's a **cute little bird**. Poor little fella must have blown out of his nest."

Sure enough, there was an **empty nest** on a branch high above us.

"Now, off you go, bird, **fly back** to the tree," said Lizzie. "**Flap** those wings. Flap and flap, and **fly through the sky!**"

What do we do now? I thought to myself. We can't leave this **poor little guy** without a way to get back to his nest.

We needed someone who could **climb** trees . . . and sausage dogs just **don't climb** trees.

"Kev!" I said. "You're a cat! **Cats can climb stuff!** Can you take him back up?"

No. I guess he had a point.

"Don't give me to the cat," said Birdy.
"He'll **eat** me!"

NO WAY!

"Don't worry, Birdy," said Kev, "I'm more of a **pie** and **chips** and **doughnut** kind of guy. Plus I've had breakfast already."

We all turned to Lizzie.

You might be thinking . . . **Yes**, great idea, **Lizards can climb trees**, right? Why doesn't the lizard take the baby bird back up?

Well . . . here's something you need to know about Lizzie.

She's **one tough lizard**. She can take on the **biggest bully** in the universe.

YOU WANT A PIECE OF ME? COME ON! MAKE IT SNAPPY!

She'll **eat anything**.
Even stuff Kev won't eat.

BIG BUG
BURGER

BUT when it comes to **heights**...

she **hates** them! You won't find Lizzie **up** a tree. Ever!

In fact, she even gets **dizzy** when she wears **high-heels**!

"You know I'm **not** going up there," said Lizzie.

"Well, what do we do?" I asked. "We can't just leave the baby bird here by himself . . ."

THREE

YOU'RE **VERY HEAVY** FOR A LITTLE BIRDY.

YOU'RE FUNNY-LOOKING FOR A LIZARD.

None of us could **figure out** a way to get the bird back up to his nest, so we decided to go and **find his mum.**

I was hoping to **fly my kite** today, but that would have to wait.

"So what does your mum **look like**?" I asked Birdy.

"I don't know," he said. "Like me, but **bigger.**"

Normally I'd be able to **use my nose** to track down his mum, but it was still **completely stuffy**!

SNIFF!

Nothing!

"Hey, everyone!" Birdy suddenly shouted. "That's my mum over there!"

We all looked where Birdy was pointing. We saw just a **tiny shape** of another bird on the **other side of the river**, past the **waterpark**.

"Take me to her, Lizard Lady!" Birdy ordered.

"Quick!" I said. "Let's **follow** her!"

Problem was, between us and Birdy's mother was

a **BIG** river.

It wasn't like I could **doggie paddle** across with everyone on my back...

A very **BAD** idea!

There was a **pair of oars** by the river, but **no boat** . . . What could we do?

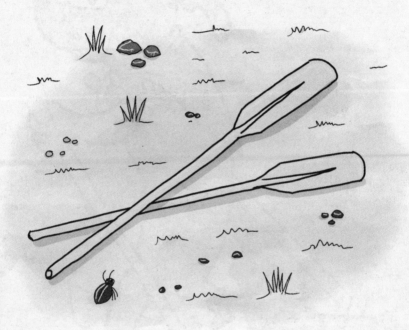

We needed something **big**.

Something that would **float**.

We needed . . .

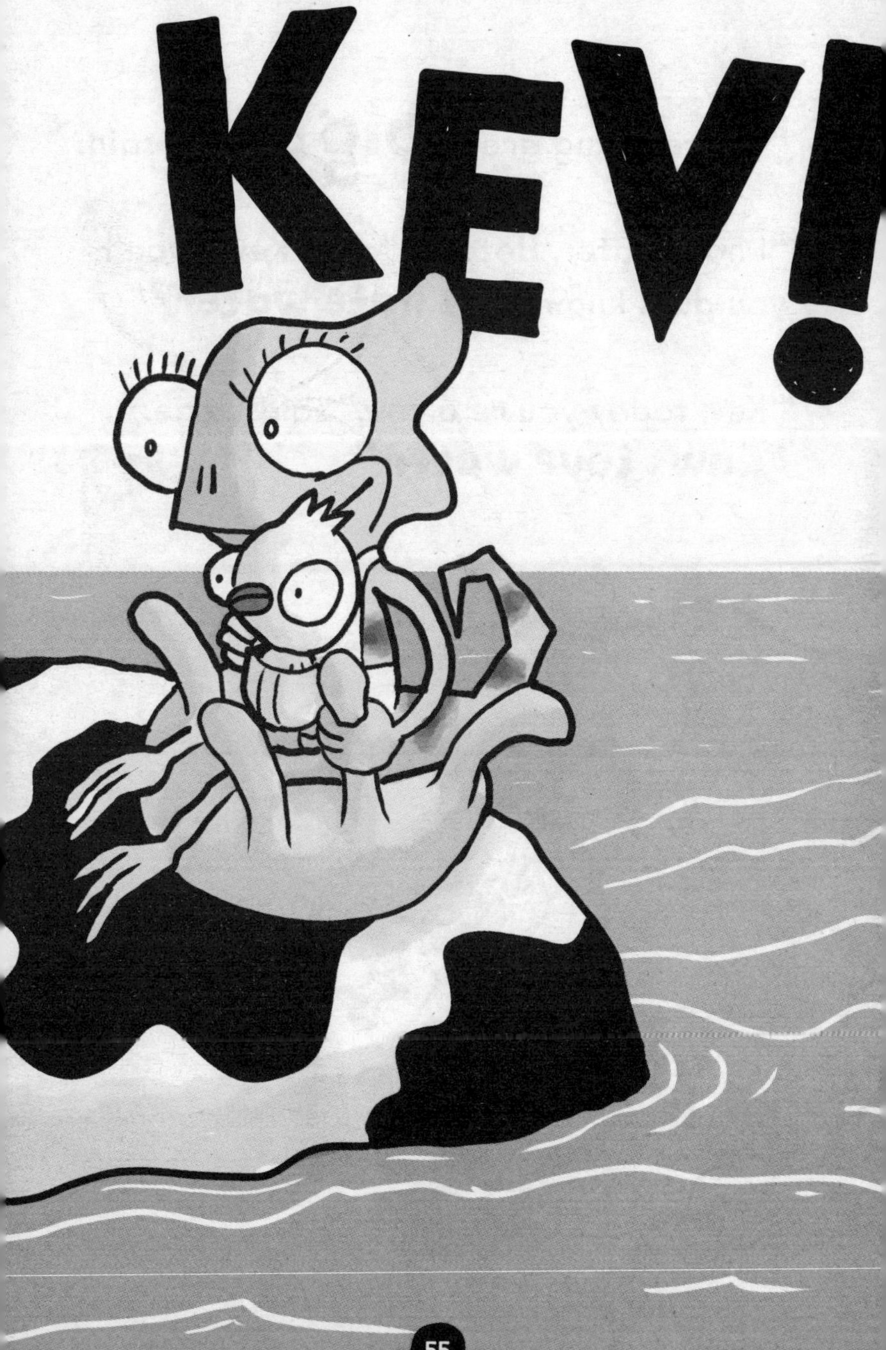
KEV!

"You're doing great, **big guy!**" I said.

"I hate water, Hotdog!" said Kev. "Don't you guys know **cats hate water?**"

"Kev, today you're a cow," said Lizzie. **"Cows love water."**

"Oh," said Kev. "OK then."

My arms might be **little**, but man they can **row!** In no time we were almost halfway across the river.

We could almost see the other side when Kev started complaining about a **REALLY bad smell.**

My nose was still **blocked**, so I couldn't **smell** a thing!

"Kev, have you been **eating beans** again?" Kev had a bad bean habit, so I had to check it wasn't **him** he was smelling!

"No, I haven't had any beans!" he said.

So what was that **terrible smell**?

"It's . . . it's . . ." Kev began.

"It's—

POOP!"

shrieked Lizzie. "It's poop! The baby bird has pooped himself! I hate **bird poop!**"

"**Hey!**" Birdy cried. "You just need to **change my nappy!**"

"Oh, no," said Lizzie. "I didn't sign up for nappy changing. I'm a **poop-free zone.**"

"Please," begged Birdy. "It was just a little accident. I can't help that I'm still a baby!"

We were **wobbling** so much that Kev was about to tip over!

WHO OAH!

"Please, Lizzie, it's just **a tiny bit of bird poop**," I said. "We need your help!"

"All right, all right!" said Lizzie. "I'll do it."

"Hey," I said, "where'd my **scarf** go?"

TA-DA!

"Now let's hurry up and **find that bird**."

FOUR

Finally, we were back on land again. "That was **awesome**, Kev," I said, patting my friend on the back. "Not only do you make a **great cow**, but you also make a **great raft!**"

At that moment we were interrupted by a whole bunch of—

QUACK!

QUACK!

"Hotdog!" said Lizzie. "We've **found** the mother! **Hey you!**" she yelled, reaching for the **biggest** duck.

The **duck** turned around. Lizzie took off the **baby carrier** and popped it on her.

"I believe this little birdy belongs to **you**."

QUACK?

"Lizard lady, that's **not** my mum!" said Birdy.

"Yes, it is!" said Lizzie. "You've just been **apart** for so long that you've forgotten what she looks like."

"I know my own mum," said the baby bird. "And this is **NOT** her."

LISTEN HERE...

"It's got **feathers**," said Lizzie. "It's got **wings**. It's **gotta be your mum.**"

"You've got **Legs** and the cat's got **Legs**, that doesn't mean he's your mum," said Birdy.

The little guy **had a point!**

"Excuse me, duck," I said. "Is this
baby bird yours?"

"I'm **afraid not**," she replied.
"At least, I don't think I'm
missing anyone."

1, 2, 3, 4, 5 . . .

"I told you so," said the baby bird. "Hey, there's my mum over there! She's heading down that path!"

Again, we all looked up for Birdy's mum. I saw a **flash of feathers** flying down towards a **big barn**.

She was headed for
the **berry farm**!

"Let's go!"

FIVE

We reached the **farm** and stood by the gates, wondering how in the world we were going to get **inside**. We needed a **pig**, or a **horse**, or a **sheep**, or a . . .

FARM ANIMALS
ONLY

COW!

Kev snuck inside with a bunch of **real cows**.

MOO!

And it wasn't long before he came back!

LOOK!
I FOUND YOUR MUM!

"That's **not** my mum!" said Birdy.

"Huh?" said Kev. "Are you **sure?** It has to be!'

"Here we go again," said Birdy. "I know what my mum looks like, and that chicken is **not** her! **Not even close!** My mum looks much less ... like him."

"I'm **not** a chicken, thanks very much. I'm a **rooster**," said the rooster. "I'm a **karate-chopping rooster!**"

HI-YA!

That rooster was one **really tough** guy!

"We're **never** going to find her," said Birdy. **"Eep, eep, eep,"** he sobbed.

"Of course we will," said Lizzie. "Look at this **amazing team** that's on the case. What could possibly go wrong?"

Just then I saw another **flash of feathers** in the sky.

"Wait a minute," I said. "Is that her up there?"

MAMA!

She was heading towards the **beach**!

"Come on guys, let's go!"

SIX

"That's **my mum** up there!" said Birdy. He was pointing all the way up to the **Lighthouse**.

I could just see the bird right next to the lighthouse window.

I looked at my friends. We were all **exhausted**.

Especially Kev.

JUST LEAVE
ME HERE...

Lizzie looked **tired**, too. She'd been carrying Birdy around **all day!**

We'd **never** make it up the lighthouse stairs in time to catch the mother.

So how could we make it there **faster**?

We needed a **helicopter** or a **hot air balloon** ... or ... or ...

a kite!

HEEEEELLLLLLLLLP...

91

MEEEEEEEEEEE

A great **gust of wind** sent us **soaring** up to the lighthouse. It was **awesome!**

"So this is what it's like to **fly**!" said Birdy.

"Get ready to drop!" I called out to everyone as we neared the top of the lighthouse.

"Ready, set . . ."

We landed with a **loud splat!**

I was **untangling** myself from my kite when I heard Lizzie **cry** out.

"FINALLY!" she said. "We **found** your mum, Birdy!"

I turned around.

YOUR MUM!

"She's **not** my mum!" Birdy shouted.
"You really don't know much about
birds, do you?"

"No, no, you're just confused because
your mum is wearing this **funny
dinner suit**," said Lizzie.

"It's not a suit, I'm a penguin," said
the penguin. "And I am **not** that
baby's mother."

"And what's a penguin doing all the way up here?" said Lizzie.

"What does it look like I'm doing?" said the penguin. "I'm up here for the **photos**!"

SAY CHEESE!

We must have frightened Birdy's real mum away, because there was no-one else around aside from a **busload** of **penguins**.

FLASH! FLASH! FLASH! FLASH! FLASH!

Slowly, we made our way back down the stairs to the beach.

Birdy was looking **really sad**.

We'd come so close to Birdy's mum three times. I normally solved problems, but I was running **out of ideas!**

I MISS MY MUM...

Lizzie looked really tired.

"Lizzie, want me to take him for a little while?" I asked.

"Yes, **please**. Thanks, Hotdog."

I took the baby sling. As I picked Birdy up, his little head feathers **tickled** my nose.

A—

OOOH!

The **enormous** sneeze completely **unblocked** my nose. I could **smell** again!

"I can smell the **sea**, I can smell **fish and chips . . .**

But best of all, I can smell **pine and berries** and the **river**! And I'm sure that's the smell of **Birdy's mum!**"

I followed my nose away from the **beach** . . . where we'd flown the kite.

Past the berries and the **farm** . . . Around the **river** . . . and all the way back to the **big pine tree**, where our **adventure** began.

Suddenly, over at the **waterpark**, I saw something that looked just like Birdy, but bigger! It must have been Birdy's mum!

She was perched on top of the **mini waterslide**!

It was a **long tube** that went around and **waaaay** up high.

I looked over at the stairs to the top, but the gate was bolted shut.

We had to find someone who could **climb up** that tube. It **was not** going to be easy.

We needed someone who would **try** their hardest to make it. Someone who wouldn't give up. Someone like **me!**

"OK, Birdy," I said, "I'm going to get you to your mum!'

It was **REALLY** tricky getting up the slide!

There were lots of tough *twists* and *turns*.

But we finally made it to the top. **Phew!**

Just as I was about to climb out of the slide, Birdy's mum flew off again! **Can you believe it?!**

But I still wasn't going to give up! This was our chance! We had to **keep trying!**

I climbed out as **fast** as I could, and then we both yelled with all our might!

MUUUMMYY!!!

And guess what? She must have heard us because she turned around!

YAY!

I was so tired, I leaned back and **slipped!**

Birdy and I slid all the way back down the slide!

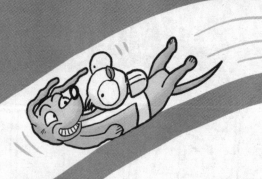

SPLASH!

Lizzie and Kev **helped** us out of the water.

MAMA!

WINSTON!

"I've been **looking for you everywhere**," said the bird. "What happened to you?"

The bird turned to me and Lizzie and Kev. She looked very confused.

"A big gust of wind **blew me** out of the nest," said Birdy.

"He can't fly yet," said Lizzie, "so he was **stuck** on the ground."

"All by himself," I added.

UH-HUH.

"So we went looking for you," I explained. "To get him back to you."

"Mama! I **missed** you so much!" said Winston. "These are my new friends, and we had the **BEST DAY EVER!**"

THE BEST DAY EVER?

"We went **rafting**," he said, "we went to the **farm**, we **flew a kite**! We had so much **fun**!"

"I think this calls for a **celebration**," said Kev.

"Well, you did return Winston to me safe and sound. I think I owe you a party," said Mama Bird.

"With cake?" said Kev.

OF COURSE! THANK YOU SO MUCH FOR LOOKING AFTER MY BABY!

What a day!

We found Winston's mum, flew a kite and even made some new friends. I couldn't wait for our **next adventure!**

WHAT A TEAM!

ONE

Hi, I'm Hotdog. I'm a **sausage** dog. I'm like an ordinary dog that's been s-t-r-e-t-c-h-e-d.

You must meet my
two **best** friends.

There's **Lizzie
the lizard.** →

And **Kev
the cat.**

It's Kev's **birthday** today and we're throwing him a **surprise party** at my place!

SHHH! DON'T TELL HIM!

Kev doesn't have a clue! We've been working really hard on our **party planning**. We have loads of **food**, **games** and other **fun** things!

We have . . .

lots of **sprinkles** ready for **fairy bread**!

Corn kernels for **popcorn**!

And a **HUGE** wobbly cake made out of **jelly**!

We've chosen some of our **favourite games** to play . . . like **Pin the Tail on the Donkey.**

Kev really likes **Lollies** so Lizzie's been working on a **huge CHICKEN piñata** for him.

A **piñata** is like a big box made out of paper that you fill with **Lollies**. Then you hit it with a stick while wearing a blindfold! And **sweets rain down!**

But what Kev likes the most of all . . . is **dinosaurs**!

I had blown up heaps of **balloons**, and Lizzie wanted to make them look like **dinosaurs** by adding **eyes and teeth.**

ALMOST DONE.

They looked **really scary!**

"Great job, Lizzie," I said. "Let's hide those away in the closet for now . . ."

Best of all, Lizzie was going to perform some **magic**!

She'd been practising her tricks for weeks.

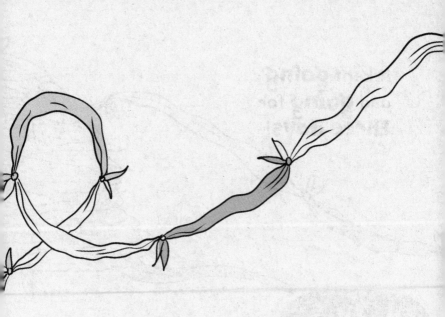

Like the **never-ending hanky!**

She also tried the **pulling-a-coin-from-behind-my-ear** trick.

But Lizzie's **best trick** was . . .

SAWING A
HOTDOG
IN HALF!

Trust me, I was **NOT HAPPY** about
that one at first!

But once Lizzie explained to me how it would work, I agreed to do it.

For Kev!

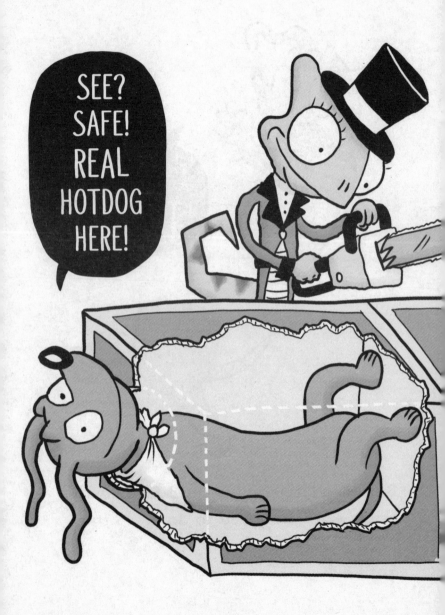

He was going to **Love** it!

It had been **REALLY hard** keeping
Kev away from all of our party planning.

KEV! LOOK OVER THERE! A MEAT PIE!

Especially today, as it was his **birthday** and we hadn't even wished him a **happy birthday** yet!

In fact, we'd kept him outside
all morning.

He was starting to look really sad.
Really, really sad.

That would all change as soon as we crossed off the last thing on our list of things to do.

BUY KEV'S PRESENT!

And we knew **exactly** what to get him!

TWO

Kev didn't want to stay behind, so we had to take him with us to the shops.

On the way, Lizzie leant over and whispered in my ear. "How are we going to buy his present without him **SEEING**?!"

"What did you say?" asked Kev.

Lizzie's good at making things up, so she told Kev, "Have you ever seen a **polar bear PEEING?**"

IT PROBABLY COMES OUT LIKE ICE CUBES!

Lizzie and I both laughed.

HA HA HA HA HA HA!

We'd only taken a few more steps before
Lizzie started whispering again.

I don't think Lizzie knows how to whisper
properly. She just **shouts** while
covering her mouth.

"Hotdog," she said, "it could **ruin** the **SURPRISE**!"

"What did you say?" Kev asked.

Lizzie thought quickly and then told Kev, "Umm, I think I've got something in **MY EYES**!"

"There sure is something in there," said Kev, "... **your eyeballs**!"

Kev thought that was a **great joke**,
and we all laughed.

Phew, Kev still had **no idea** about the
party! I left Lizzie outside the shops,
trying to distract Kev, while I ran inside
to find the **ROARING DINO BIKE!**

LOOK AT ME, LOOK AT ME, NOTHING TO SEE, LOOK AT MEEEEEE!

There was only **one bike left!**

RING DINO BIKE!

I grabbed the last one **just in time . . .**

not knowing that **someone else really** wanted that bike too!

I felt a **bit bad** that I'd taken the last bike, but I had **bigger** things to worry about. Like, how to hide the bike and get it home!

Wrap it in toilet paper!

"Wow," said Kev. "You must **really need** toilet paper."

"You never know when you gotta go," I said with a shrug.

Lizzie had something slung over her shoulder.

"What's that?" I asked her.

"Me and Kev found a pair of **roller-skates** in the bin! Someone had thrown them out!"

SEE?

"What are you going to do with those?"
I asked.

"You never know when you **gotta roll**," said Lizzie.

Just as we turned the corner towards my place, I thought I saw something that looked like the **rooster** and **donkey** behind us.

But it was just a

funny-Looking
bush.

Besides, what would they be doing

following
us home?

THREE

Kev was **NOT** happy about waiting outside again.

"We just need you to, um, watch the trolley while we take the, um, toilet paper inside," said Lizzie.

"That's right," I agreed. "We won't be long. I promise."

As we carried the box inside I heard Kev say to himself, "I can't believe my **best friends** didn't even remember my **birthday . . .**"

We had to **hurry**! It was terrible seeing Kev **so sad**!

SOB.

Once we were inside we tied a **ribbon around the box**. Then we **ducked down and hid** behind the couch.

"Kev!" I shouted. "You can come in now!"

The door slowly opened and Kev shuffled in. "Where is everyone?" he grumbled. "Looks like I'm on my own again—"

Kev was **so surprised** he jumped back like a **startled frog!**

"Happy birthday, big guy!" Lizzie sang out.

"Wow!" said Kev, "I thought you'd forgotten!"

"We'd **never forget** your birthday," I said, giving Kev a hug.

"NEVER, you crazy cat," said Lizzie. "We've been working **FOR DAYS** on making sure you have the **greatest party EVER!"**

"That's right!" I said. "Now let's start with your **present**!"

"The **toilet paper** was for me all along?" said Kev.

"Don't be silly," said Lizzie. "Your present's underneath the toilet paper."

Kev ripped off the **ribbon** and **tore apart the box.**

YOU GOT ME THE ROARING DINO BIKE! I CAN'T BELIEVE IT!

Kev **jumped** right on the bike and started **zooming** around the room. He was popping **wheelies, spinning around** and **roaring like a T-rex!**

ROAR!

It was **awesome**. Actually, it was
ROARSOME!

"Let me on!" yelled Lizzie.

Kev skidded by, and Lizzie jumped on.
As they **zipped away**, I thought I saw
the **ROOSTER** and **DONKEY** watching
them through the window.

In fact, **I DID** see the **ROOSTER** and **DONKEY** watching through the window.

They had their eyes on **Kev's** new bike!

And they were trying to **get in**!

This was meant to be the **greatest birthday party ever**. I couldn't have one **rude rooster** and one **cranky donkey** ruining it! We'd made Kev really sad this morning, so now we had to make it up to him!

Somehow I needed to get rid of those guys without Kev finding out what was going on!

It was going to be one **tough mission**. But I'm **always up for anything!**

FOUR

Kev was so happy when he saw his cake! "**Jelly!** My **favourite!**" he said.

DROOOL

He was so distracted by the **wobbling jelly** that it gave me a chance to pull Lizzie aside.

"Lizzie," I whispered, "we have trouble. **Rooster** and **Donkey** are outside. They followed us home from the shops. I bought the last bike and they were **NOT HAPPY**."

I THINK THEY'RE GOING TO TRY AND PINCH KEV'S BIKE!

Lizzie looked **real** mad.

YOU DO NOT WANT TO MESS WITH AN ANGRY LIZARD!

"What did you say?" asked Kev.

"Um," said Lizzie, "when it comes to making cakes, Hotdog's a **WIZARD!**"

All of a sudden we were interrupted by a loud **thud** on the roof.

"What was that?" said Kev.

It must have been those **pesky** guys up there, trying to get in through the chimney!

THUD!
THUD!

I had to **think fast**!

"It must be the, um, **pigeons** back again," I said. "They love hanging out on our roof."

THEY MUST BE SOME BIG PIGEONS!

"HUGE," I said. "They spend a lot of time at the **gym** working out."

I needed to get Kev away from the fireplace!

"Kev," I said, "why don't you go and help Lizzie cook the **popcorn**?"

"Ooh, **popcorn**, my favourite!" said Kev. Kev had **a lot** of favourites when it came to food.

I watched as Lizzie grabbed the huge sack of corn kernels ... and poured the **WHOLE LOT** into the pot.

THAT SHOULD BE ENOUGH!

I thought it was **waaaaay** too much, but I had bigger things to worry about!

The **thudding** above was getting **Louder** ... I was pretty sure **Rooster** and **Donkey** were moments away from landing inside!

I needed to do something! **Quick!**

I grabbed the jelly cake and shoved it under the chimney.

I hid **under** the table, waiting for the rooster and donkey to arrive.

The **rooster** landed first.

SPLAT!

Then the **donkey**!

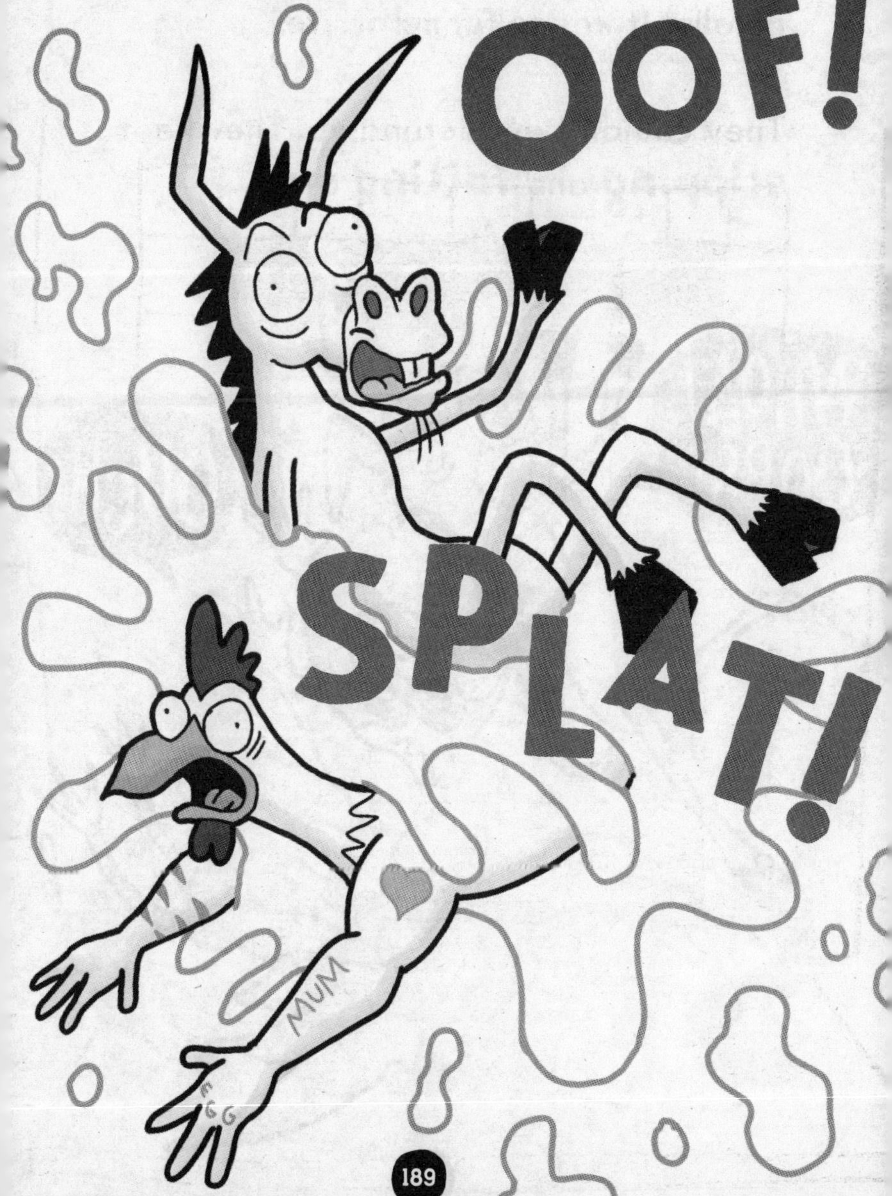

They were both completely **COVERED** in jelly! It was so funny!

They couldn't even stand up. They kept **slipping** and **falling** over!

"Get up and **fetch that bike**, Donkey!" screeched the rooster to the donkey.

"**YOU** get up and get it, Rooster!" said the donkey, who was slipping like a giraffe on ice!

Just when I thought it couldn't get **any funnier**, Rooster fell onto the table...

... and emptied the **sprinkles** all over himself and his buddy!

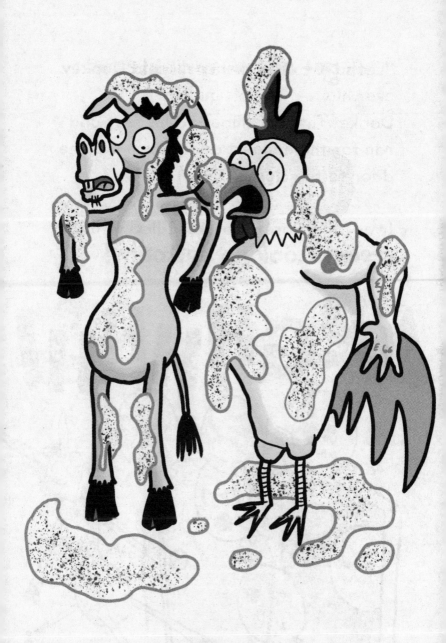

"Let's **get out** of here!" said Donkey.

Donkey finally climbed to his feet and ran for the nearest door, which was the door to the closet!

It was the closet that was filled with the **creepy-looking balloons!**

ARGHHHH!

Donkey screamed!

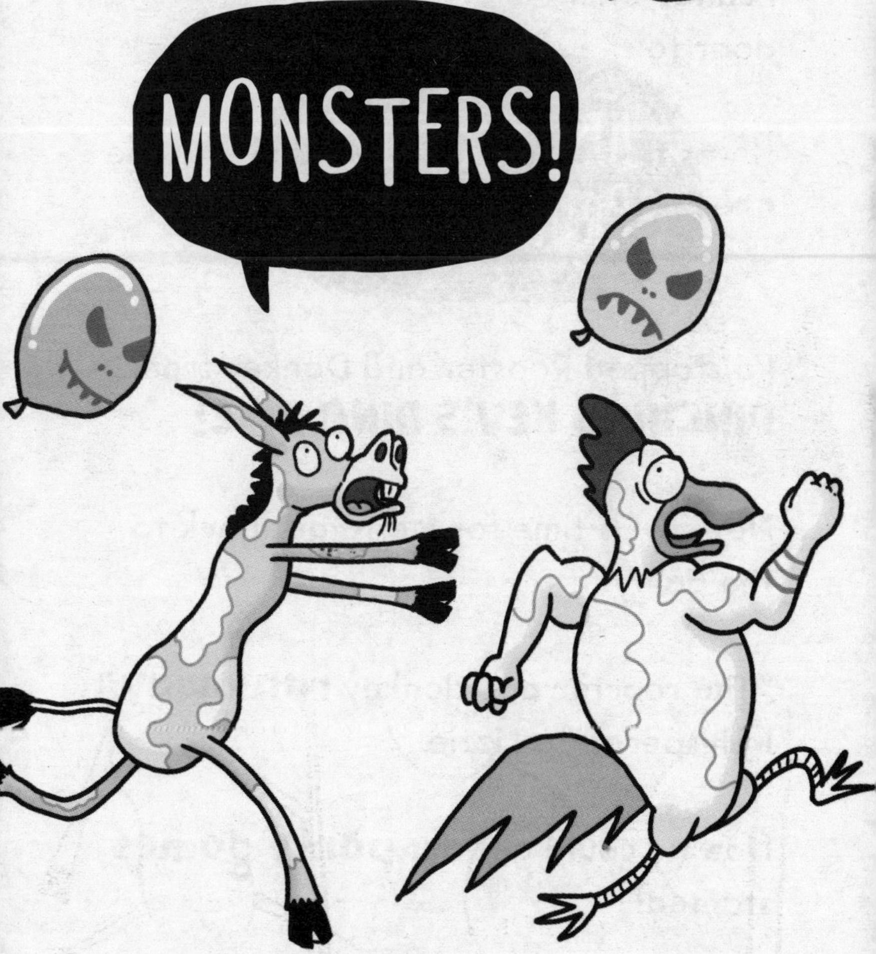

"Everything OK in there?" yelled out Lizzie.

I called back—

JUST A LITTLE SPRINKLE SPILL!

I'd stopped Rooster and Donkey from **PINCHING KEV'S DINO BIKE!**

Now it was time for me to get back to the party!

"The rooster and donkey **ran away**," I whispered to Lizzie.

Now we could get our **party games** started!

. . . OR SO I THOUGHT!

They hadn't gone anywhere!

I was just getting our **first game** ready when . . .

SCREECH!
ZOOOM!

I turned back around and
the bike was gone!

SMELL
YOU
LATER!

Kev looked **sadder** than ever!

THEY PINCHED MY BIKE?!

"Ooh, they have messed with the **WRONG party!**" said Lizzie.

I couldn't let them get away. I had to come up with an idea to chase them down, **fast!**

"Don't worry, Kev!" I said. "Lizzie, hand me your **skates!**"

FIVE

THIS IS AWESOME!

We were **FLYING** down the street
after the robbers!

It was **SO** easy to follow Rooster and Donkey ... all we had to do was follow the trail of **SPRINKLES**!

We **zipped** down the pavement,

skidded around the river,

jumped over a few **terrified turtles**...

Then I saw our chance. **A BIG BEND** in the road.

I just needed one **big push** to reach them!

"You can do it, Hotdog!" Kev and Lizzie shouted out.

My legs skated as fast as they possibly could! I **HAD** to get that bike back for my friend!

We sped up like a **racing car**!

We were **SO** close! Rooster and Donkey were distracted by us and they didn't see the **TREE STUMP** in front of them.

They **hit the stump** and went
FLYING through the air. They **flipped**
and **tumbled** and **landed** . . .

This was **our chance** to take back the bike!

We waved **goodbye** to Rooster and Donkey.

SIX

Once we made it back home . . .

. . . we decided to **let the games** begin!

Kev was up first for **Pin the Tail on the Donkey!**

We blindfolded him and spun him around. Then Kev wobbled towards the poster on the wall.

Kev pushed the pin **HARD** into the donkey poster.

"Oops," said Kev, after taking off his blindfold. "That's not where a **tail** goes!"

"My turn!" shouted Lizzie.

We blindfolded Lizzie and spun her around **really** fast.

Lizzie got her pin in the donkey's **arm**!

When it was my turn, I pinned the donkey's **foot**!

Oops.

222

Out the corner of my eye, I suddenly spotted **ROOSTER**, crouched behind the couch in the other room!

He was **back!** I couldn't believe it! And he was staring at the donkey poster on the wall.

"DONKEY!?!" I heard Rooster cry. "What have they done to you?!"

From where he was hiding, Rooster must have thought the **donkey** on the **poster** was his **buddy**!

"Now let's try the piñata!" said Lizzie.

"Great chicken piñata!" said Kev.

THANKS...
NOW LET'S
DESTROY IT!

We blindfolded Kev again, spun him around ... and he let loose on the chicken!

WHACK!
WHACK!

POW!

"Go Kev!" cheered Lizzie.

But then, out the corner of my eye, I spotted **DONKEY**, crouched behind a chair in the other room!

Donkey was back, too! He was staring at the **chicken piñata**!

"Rooster?!" he cried. "What have they done to you?!"

From where he was hiding, **Donkey** must have thought the **chicken piñata** was his **buddy!**

POW! WHACK!

Surely that would send him running away!

Kev was **WHACKING** and **BOPPING** the piñata so hard that lollies started spilling everywhere!

"And finally, Kev," said Lizzie, "it's time for your **BIG BIRTHDAY MAGIC SHOW!**"

PREPARE TO BE AMAZED!

"Assistant," said Lizzie. She was talking to me. "Please join me on the stage of **wonder**."

Kev was so excited. He **LOVED** magic tricks.

I ran up to Lizzie and climbed into the
box, carefully **tucking** my feet away.
The fake feet popped out the other side.

I had a quick look around to see whether I could spot Rooster and Donkey anywhere. But they were **nowhere** to be found.

The **dino bike** was still safe.

Had they finally **given up** and gone away? Surely we'd **scared** them off!

"Now," said Lizzie, "I will **SAW THIS HOTDOG IN HALF!**"

Lizzie pulled out her chainsaw.

Lizzie sawed right through the box, just like we'd practised.

In moments, the box was in half!

Lizzie pulled the halves apart – me on one side, my fake feet on the other!

It had worked!

Kev cheered louder than I'd ever heard him cheer before.

TA-DA!

"Great job, Lizzie!" said Kev. "Hotdog's now a **HALFDOG!**"

All of a sudden we heard two **ENORMOUS** screams! One coming from our left, and the other from our right.

Donkey and Rooster ran towards each other from either side of the room. They were **screaming** and **running** like crazy, their arms waving **wildly** in the air.

They ran so hard and so fast that they **CRASHED** right into each other!

DONK!

Was this what we needed to **FINALLY** get rid of them, **ONCE AND FOR ALL?!**

All of a sudden I noticed a weird **rattling** sound coming from the kitchen. Before I could work out what it was . . .

. . . there was a **HUGE** EXPLOSION!

We'd **completely forgotten** about the **popcorn**! It was flying everywhere!

Rooster and Donkey **BOLTED** out the front door!

FINALLY they'd had enough and run away! Phew.

"See ya," Kev called out, "wouldn't want to be ya!"

POPCORN, ANYONE?

SEVEN

Kev **LOVED** the popcorn explosion.

"First it rained lollies. Then it rained popcorn. There's food everywhere. This is a **DREAM COME TRUE!**"

Kev chomped through all the food like a lawnmower!

Before long, he had completely cleaned up the place!

WHAT A GREAT– HIC–BURP–DAY!

Lizzie and I grinned at each other. We were **so happy** Kev loved his party, and we were so happy we didn't let a **ROOSTER** and **DONKEY** ruin his day!

"You guys are the **best friends** a guy could ever have," said Kev. "Come over here and give me a hug."

HAPPY BIRTHDAY, KEV!